THE UNEXPURGATED ADVENTURES OF SHERLOCK HOLMES

BOOK 11

THE SECRET PREDICAMENT OF THE STUPID BANKER

by NP Sercombe

The un-edited manuscript originally entitled *The Adventure of the Noble Bachelor* written by Dr. John Watson and Sir Arthur Conan Doyle

Illustrations by Juliet Snape

This novel is entirely a work of fiction. The names, characters and incidents portrayed in it are the work of the author's and illustrator's imaginations. Any resemblance to actual persons, living or dead, events or localities, is entirely coincidental.

Published by EVA BOOKS 2021 – c/o Harry King Films Limited
                1&2 The Barn
                West Stoke Road
                Lavant
                n/r Chichester
                West Sussex PO18 9AA

Copyright © NP Sercombe 2021

The rights of Nicholas Sercombe to be identified as the author of this work have been asserted in accordance with the Copyright, Designs and Patents Act 1988.

A CIP catalogue record for this book is available from the British Library.

ISBN 978-1-8381045-0-4 (Hardback)

Book layout & cover design by Clare Brayshaw.

Cover illustration by Juliet Snape.

Set in Bruce Old Style.

Prepared and printed by: York Publishing Services Ltd
64 Hallfield Road, Layerthorpe, York YO31 7ZQ

Tel: 01904 431213

Website: www.yps-publishing.co.uk

All rights reserved. No part of this publication may be reproduced, stored in a retrieval system, or transmitted, in any form or by any means; by that we mean electrical, mechanical, photocopying, recording or otherwise, without the prior written permission of the publisher.

This book is sold subject to the condition that it shall not, by way of trade or otherwise, be lent, re-sold, hired out or otherwise circulated without the publisher's prior written consent in any form of binding or cover other than that in which it is published and without similar condition including this condition being imposed on the subsequent purchaser.

THE UNEXPURGATED ADVENTURES OF SHERLOCK HOLMES

Books in the Series:

A BALLS-UP IN BOHEMIA
THE MYSTERIOUS CASE OF MR. GINGERNUTS
THE CASE OF THE RANDY STEPFATHER
MY FIRST PROPER RURAL MURDER
THE ORANGES OF DEATH!
THE MAN WITH THE HAIRY FACE
A GANDER AT THE BLUE CARBUNCLE
THE SPECKLED BAND SPECULATION
THE ADVENTURE OF THE ENGINEER'S TONGUE
THE MYSTERIOUS MARRIAGE OF THE GAY BACHELOR
THE SECRET PREDICAMENT OF THE STUPID BANKER

Nicholas Sercombe is a writer and producer for film and television. He has been lucky enough to work in comedy for most of the Holocene period with some of the greatest performers and writers. He is most comfortable when reading Conan Doyle and even happier when re-writing these extraordinarily entertaining stories by Dr. John Watson.

Juliet Snape studied illustration at Cambridge School of Art and Central St. Martins. She has illustrated over 100 books and her work has been published around the world.

She is a fan of Sherlock Holmes – her father even lived in Baker Street – and, in the words of Conan Doyle, she is *"naturally gravitated to London, that great cesspool into which all the loungers and idlers of the Empire are irresistibly drained."* She lives in London and loves sketching, finding inspiration all around her. She has two children, both successful creatives.

For people who can manage mind over matter

The Secret Predicament
of the Stupid Banker

(published in The Strand in May 1892 with the title
THE ADVENTURE OF THE BERYL CORONET
by Dr. Watson and Arthur Conan Doyle)

'Holmes,' said I, as I stood one morning in our bow-window looking down the street, 'here is a madman coming along. It seems rather sad that his relatives should allow him to come out alone.'

My friend rose lazily from his armchair and stood with his hands in the pockets of his dressing-gown looking over my shoulder. It was a bright, crisp March morning in 1891 and the unseasonal snow of the day before still lay deep upon the ground, shimmering brightly in the wintry sun. Down the centre of Baker Street it had been ploughed into a brown crumbly band by the traffic, but at either side and on the heaped-up edges of the footpaths it still lay as white as when it fell. I could still make out the dainty footprints of the two girls who had just departed, a fine duo of trollops supplied by Mother Kelly as part of her new knocking-shop innovation of a home-delivery service. And thank goodness for it, because the snowstorm had been so intense the night before that the great detective had refused to leave the apartment to patronise the Kingly Street establishment for his weekly routine of female distraction. As a doctor, I knew about his physiological needs and the frequency thereof; as a friend and co-resident of 221B Baker Street, I knew that this was every six days, and even a delay of one could affect his mental condition so severely that he would become impossible to live with. For instance, whenever we reached day seven, habitually he would reach for the stash of cocaine and send himself into orbit around Jupiter. Then, even worse still, he would caress Horatio, his beloved violin, and play the most melancholic of Scottish *études* ever composed – i.e. *Folk Songs from tha' Glescae Slums*. And that is precisely what happened last night. Oh, misery! As soon as Horatio came out of his case I rattled my mind for emergency inspiration. I prayed to the gods and Zeus sent me a thunderbolt from Mount Olympus. All of a sudden, I remembered reading a notice about a new service on the members board at Mother Kelly's, only a fortnight ago.

'Holmes!' cried I, jumping up from my seat to startle my companion into hiatus. 'What about some Fanny by Gaslight?'

Sherlock Holmes dropped his bow and looked up from his music stand.

'What, pray, is Fanny by Gaslight?'

'It is a new service where the girls venture out of the Kingly Street knocking-shop to visit the customers. All we have to do is to choose our fancy and place the order by telegram.'

And, sure enough, an hour later I greeted two emissaries from Mother Kelly's. I met up with them outside, just around the corner from 221B because I knew that they would be excited and silly, and I did not dare disturb Mrs. Hudson; with two months' rent outstanding she would harangue me without mercy. I guided them up the stairs successfully, quietly giggling, had them installed in our apartment and they got down to business. We had a right old time of things, but it carried on all through the night, which was why this morning the great detective and your dutiful chronicler were hung out like the washing.

'I say,' said Holmes, taking in the condition of the snow, 'the pavement may have been scraped but it looks dangerously slippery. No wonder nobody wishes to chance their luck upon it, apart from the fellow you refer me to. He must be desperately out of sorts to risk his neck on sheet ice.'

And there was the man still walking like a madman, skating from one foot to the other but staying up on his feet. I would guess that he was about fifty. He was tall, portly, and imposing, with a massive, strongly marked face with a full beard and a commanding figure. He was dressed in a sombre yet rich style, in black frock-coat, shining hat, neat brown gaiters, and well-cut pearl-grey trousers. Yet his actions were in absurd contrast to the dignity of his dress and features, for he was running hard, with occasional little springs, such as a weary man gives who is little accustomed to set any tax upon his legs. As he ran he jerked his hands up and down, waggled his head, and writhed his face into the most extraordinary contortions.

'What on Earth can be the matter with him?' I asked. 'He is looking up at the numbers of the houses.'

'That is because he is coming here,' said Holmes, rubbing his hands with glee.

'Here? But my dear Holmes, after seven hours of Fanny by Gaslight? We are not even dressed!'

'Well, Doctor, I find that exercising my mind is more invigorating than any other part of my anatomy. That madman is coming to consult me professionally. I think that I recognise the symptoms. Ha! Did I not tell you?' As he spoke, the man, puffing and blowing, rushed at our door, and pulled at our bell until the whole house resounded with the clanging.

A few moments later he was in our room, still puffing, still gesticulating, but with so fixed a look of grief and despair in his eyes that our smiles were turned in an instant to horror and pity.

'Gentlemen,' he wheezed out, under stress. 'Your housekeeper is a strange bird indeed. She seemed to infer that I was responsible for two young women recently departed from this building. Preposterous!'

Holmes and I glanced at one another. That cat was out of the bag.

'It was all I could do to convince her otherwise,' continued the man, all sweaty and blowing. 'I told her: "No, madame, I am not a pimp! I am Alexander Holdup. I have the devil on my back right now. Just let me in so that I may see Mister Sherlock Holmes."'

Luckily, no explanation of our housekeeper's behaviour was required as he went haywire again, swaying his body and plucking out his hair like one who has been driven to the extreme limits of his reason. Holmes inclined his head, indicating I should go to his rescue. I walked over and took him gently by his sleeve

'Would you like to take this chair, Mister Holdup, and rest your feet?' I led the poor anguished chap to an easy armchair, chatting with him along the way in easy, soothing tones until he was more settled. Holmes

As a doctor, I had been trained to handle insanity with sensitivity, and the nearest weapon of convenience!

drew up his armchair with the swiftest hand to engage the man in conversation. Ah, the hound had picked up the scent of a most fascinating quarry and had perked up a great deal.

'You have come to see me to tell me your story, have you not?' said he. 'You are fatigued with your haste. Pray wait until you have recovered yourself, and then I shall be most happy to look into any little problem which you may submit to me. Watson! Would you be so good as to make use of the bell-pull and summon Mrs. Hudson? We require some breakfast.'

'Holmes, do you think that it is a good idea to disturb Mrs. Hudson?'

'But of course, I do... oh!' He had registered my head nodding in the direction of our guest in reference to what he had just told us about his doorstep interrogation. 'To hell with it, Watson! We pay our dues to live here and after such a torrid night we require drink and victuals to restore our vigour. Summon our housekeeper, that's what I say!'

When he said that we pay our dues he was factually correct, but blissfully ignorant of their frequency. Even so, I pulled the cord. I noticed that our guest had made a partial recovery; he was passing his handkerchief over his brow, getting ready to speak. I walked over to the vestibule thinking it would be the best strategy to cut off Mrs. Hudson at the door, thus subduing her imminent enquiry about Fanny by Gaslight and reducing the chance of potential embarrassment in front of our guest. I leaned up against the wall, my hands behind my back, and reminisced about the sweet memories of the previous evening. Then, I weighed up the pros and cons of a visit to Mother Kelly's in Kingly

Street versus the experience of Fanny by Gaslight; the former being one of social ambience, keen anticipation, multiple choice and bailing out upon satiation; the latter being domestic familiarity, anticipation of (and gratitude for) delivery, and having the tarts on tap throughout the night. Both of them had their merits but the latter was very tiring and the process of smuggling the chits in and out of the building without detection by our landlady was a major consideration for future bookings. My thoughts were interrupted by Mr. Holdup, who was just starting his story.

'No doubt you think me preposterously mad?'

'I see that you have had some great trouble,' responded Holmes.

'God knows I have! A trouble which is enough to unseat my reason, so sudden and so terrible is it. It is preposterous! Public disgrace I might have faced, although I am a man whose character has never yet borne a stain. Private affliction also is the lot of every man; but the two coming together, and in so frightful a form, have been enough to shake my very soul. Besides, it is not I alone. The very noblest in the land may suffer, unless some way be found, out of this horrible affair.'

As I waited by the door, digesting this gentleman's opening gambit, all I could think of was "the noblest in the land..." coming up once again in one of our investigations. Why oh why did all of our clients have a claim to be the noblest in the land?

'Pray compose yourself, sir,' said Holmes, 'and let me have a clear account of who you are, and what it is that has befallen you.'

There was a knock at the door. I opened it ever so slightly, so that Holmes may not be disturbed, but Mrs. Hudson pushed against it gently. When I resisted she gave it a shove. My resistance gave way. However, she knew that we had a client in conference, so she stood her ground.

'I say, Charlotte, dear...' Her eyes narrowed instantly. I started again. 'I say, Mrs. Hudson,' said I, oiling effusively, 'would it be possible for Sherlock Holmes and me to offer breakfast to our guest?'

She walked a step closer and thrust her hand out to me.

'Rent!'

'Ahhh!' whispered I. 'I was hoping to avoid an awkward situation like this. I don't have it actually upon my person right now. Well, certainly not in this dressing-gown, nor at this very moment, or at this particular time, and OWWW!'

My involuntary ejaculation was caused by the rent collector's hand flying through the flaps of my dressing-gown with military precision. Her fingers clamped onto my rent guarantor in a vice-like grip. I had nowhere to go!

'You look frightened, Doctor.' She locked her eyes onto mine with a look of determination. 'Maybe after last night's activities you cannot raise any priapic strength?'

Dammit! Now she wanted her revenge. But after last night's torrid activities, what could I muster that could go even halfway towards satisfying her ravenous appetite?* Her fingers wound tighter, gripping harder,

---

* see *A Gander at the Blue Carbuncle*

her eyes slightly glazed, her face taking on a bemused smile. I knew that look well enough to know that she was in need of me but also I detected some added menace. My goodness she could be jealous! She gave an impatient tug. 'Well, Doctor?'

'Mrs. Hudson! I cannot possibly leave the apartment. We are entertaining the noblest of clients! Please, have a heart.'

'Tsk! He is far from being a noble. He is a banker.' And suddenly she reverted to her sunnier self. 'Hmm...' mused she, 'a banker?' She cocked her head to this revelation, 'which means that he is in the business of lending money. And he will have money.' She let go of her hostage. 'Which means he can afford to pay you. And he may be useful to me...' She was in deep pontification. I raised my eyes to the ceiling, seeking some obedience from my original request for food.

'Breakfast? Yes, of course.'

She turned on her heel and departed. I closed the door. I pondered to myself for a moment, dismissed it as trivial, and ambled back into the apartment just as our guest was pocketing his handkerchief.

'My name is probably familiar to your ears. I am Alexander Holdup...'

Who?

'...of Holdup & Stevenson, of Threadneedle Street.'

Ah! Even I had heard of that firm. They were bankers – merchant bankers – shysters – but what an unfortunate name Holdup was for the occupation he had chosen. Just imagine if he had gone into business with Mr. Stickemup. Or Mr. Stockings?

'The name is indeed well known to me,' said Holmes, just as I drew up the raspberry damask Savonarola to them and parked my posterior.

'Are you a nobleman?' I enquired.

'Shut up, Watson!' hissed Holmes. 'We are about to have a story told to us by the senior partner in the second largest banking concern in the City of London.'

'Right-ho, Holmes. Please ignore my interruption, Mister Holdup.'

'Thank you, Doctor Watson. I feel that time is of value. That is why I hastened here when the police inspector suggested that I should secure your co-operation.'

'Which policeman was that?' asked Holmes.

'Inspector Gregson. Is that of importance, Mister Holmes?'

'Yes, it is of paramount importance for me to know the source of referral amongst all of the Scotland Yard detectives. Then, I have the chance to assess their capabilities.'

'Sherlock Holmes and I like to know which of them is currently the more stupid. We have an unwritten league-table.'

'That is preposterous, sir!'

'Ha!' The good Doctor is correct, but he puts things more bluntly than I,' said Holmes suavely. 'Pray continue with your story, Mister Holdup.'

'I came to Baker Street by the Underground, and hurried from there on foot, for the cabs go slowly through this snow. That is why I was out of breath, for I am a man who takes very little exercise. I feel better now, and I will put the facts before you as shortly and yet clearly as I can.'

I wondered what could have happened to bring one of the most respected persons in the City of London to this most pitiable pass. I watched him brace himself to tell us his story.

'It is, of course, well known to you that in a successful banking business as much depends upon our being able to find remunerative investments for our funds, as upon our increasing our connection and the number of depositors. One of our most lucrative means of laying out money is in the shape of loans, where the security is unimpeachable. We have done a good deal in this direction during the last few years, and there are many noble families to whom we have advanced large sums upon the security of their pictures, libraries or plate.

'Yesterday morning I was seated in my office at the Bank when a card was brought to me by one of my clerks. I started when I saw the name, for it was that of none other than – well, perhaps even to you I had better say no more than that it was a name which is a household word all over the globe – one of the highest...'

'Noblest?'

'Shut up, Watson!'

'Yes. It is one of the noblest, and exalted names in England and beyond. I was overwhelmed by the honour, and attempted when he entered, to say so, but he plunged at once into business with the air of a man who wishes to hurry quickly through a disagreeable task.

'"Mister Holdup," said he. "I have been informed that you are in the habit of advancing money."'

"'The firm does so when the security is good,'" I answered.

"'It is absolutely essential to me,' said he, 'that I should have fifty thousand pounds at once. I could of course borrow so trifling a sum ten times over from my friends, but I much prefer to make it a matter of business, and to carry out that business myself. In my position you can readily understand that it is unwise to place oneself under obligation.'"

"'For how long, may I ask, do you want the sum?'"

"'Next Monday I have a large sum due to me, and I shall then most certainly repay what you advance, with whatever interest you think it is right to charge. But it is very essential to me that the money should be paid at once.'"

"'I should be happy to advance it without further parley from my own private purse,' said I, 'were it not that the strain would be rather more than it could bear. If, on the other hand, I am to do it in the name of the firm, then in justice to my partner I must insist that, even in your case, every business-like precaution should be taken.'"

What an oiler this banker fellow was! "My *private purse*..." and "even in *your case*...". I had taken a dislike to this man. He bore the odour of a fair-weather friend, a man who could never be wholly trusted.

'Then, Mister Holmes,' continued Mr. Holdup, 'that distinguished fellow raised up a square, black morocco case which he had laid beside the chair. "You have doubtless heard of the beryl coronet?"' enquired he.

'One of the most precious public possessions of the Empire,' stated Holmes.

'Precisely, Mister Holmes.'

'Who is this Beryl?' said I, with complete confidence.

This time Holmes didn't tell me to keep quiet; he just clapped his hands in anger.

'It is a very precious jewel, Doctor Watson!' wailed Mr. Holdup. 'Anyway, this chap opened the case, and there, embedded on soft, flesh-coloured velvet lay the magnificent piece of jewellery which he had named. "There are thirty-nine enormous beryls," said he, "and the price of the gold chasing is incalculable. The lowest estimate would put the worth of the coronet at double the sum for which I have asked. I am prepared to leave it with you as my security."'

'I took the precious case into my hands and looked in some perplexity from it to my illustrious client.'

'"You doubt its value?"' he asked.

'"Not at all. I only doubt..."'

'"The propriety of my leaving it. You may set your mind at rest about that. I should not dream of doing so were it not absolutely certain that I should be able in four days to reclaim it. It is a pure matter of form. Is the security sufficient?"'

'"Ample."'

'"You understand, Mister Holdup," continued the new client, "that I am giving you strong proof of the confidence which I have in you, founded upon all that I have heard. I rely upon you not only to be discreet and to refrain from all gossip upon the matter, but, above all, to preserve the coronet with every possible precaution, because I need not say that a great public scandal would be caused if any harm were to befall it. Any injury to it would be almost as serious as a complete loss, for there are no beryls in the world to match these, and it would be impossible to replace them. I leave it with you, however, with every confidence, and I shall call for it in person on Monday morning."'

'Seeing that my client was anxious to leave, I said no more. I called for my cashier and I ordered him to pay over fifty thousand pounds in notes. When I was alone I could not but think with some misgivings of the immense responsibility which it entailed upon me. There could be no doubt that the coronet is a jewel beloved by the nation, even though it was a personal possession. A horrible scandal would ensue if any misfortune should occur to it. I already regretted having ever consented to take charge of it. However, it was too late to alter the matter now, so I locked it up in my private safe, and turned once more to my work.'

'Indeed it is a National Treasure, with a capital N and T. Would, or could, any bank safe be strong enough to protect it, Mister Holdup?' enquired Holmes.

'Especially yours?' asked I, innocently, but realised after I spoke that I was inferring his safe to be, er, unsafe.

'Shut up, Watson!'

'Funnily enough, Doctor Watson, that is precisely the question I asked myself. When evening came, I felt that it would be imprudent to leave so precious a thing in the office behind me. Bankers' safes had been forced before now, and why should not mine be? If so, how terrible would be the position in which I should find myself! I determined, therefore, that for the next few days I would always carry the case backwards and forwards with me, so that it might never be really out of my reach. With this intention, I called a cab, and drove out to my house at Streatham, carrying the jewel with me. I did not breathe freely until I had taken it upstairs and locked it in the bureau of my dressing room.'

I glanced at Holmes in a curious way, my eyes asking him the obvious question: which establishment is more secure? (A) a bank in the heart of the City of London that has strong doors, sophisticated locks and a blistering great state-of-the-art safe at its core and armed guards; or (B) I wonder, an old wooden bureau with a lock that a child could pick in an upstairs bedroom of a house in Streatham? The great detective nodded in agreement – we were in mental harmony – but then he stopped and flicked his eyes at me. Suddenly, I realised that I was tapping my temple with my forefinger! And Mr. Holdup was staring at me! So, in a lightning moment of inspiration of avoiding embarrassment, I slapped my hand against my head.

'OUCH!' I cried. 'Damned mosquitos!' And then followed up with an unnecessary scratch and a mock look of horror at my open hand, as if I was viewing a bloody corpse.

'Really, Doctor?' drawled Holdup sarcastically. 'In March?'

'It is the Tikka mosquito. Rare in these parts. Usually found in India.' I lowered my face to my hand and pretended to lick up the pretend insect and swallow it. I smiled at Mr. Holdup, who was not looking convinced.

'Preposterous!' cried Mr. Holdup, who was glancing over to the window where the snow lay deep and crisp and even.

I had a horrible feeling that our client didn't believe a word I said about mosquitoes!

'Let us move back to this extremely interesting situation, Mister Holdup...' soothed Holmes. 'Now, please describe your household to me.'

'Ah yes, Mister Holmes, I wish you to thoroughly understand the situation. My groom and my page sleep out of the house and may be set aside altogether. I have three maid-servants who have been with me a number of years, and whose absolute reliability is quite above suspicion. Another, Lucy Parr, the second waiting-maid, has only been in my service a few months. She came with an excellent reference, however, and she has always given me satisfaction.'

Hmm! Mr. Holdup's *droit de seigneur* with the staff manifested itself. Holmes and I kept our eyes fixed firmly upon him in an unspoken treaty between us of non-ocular communication, but he picked up the scent.

'Gentlemen, please! She is a very pretty girl but I am not in the habit of molesting my maids.'

We tried to look contrite and mumbled appeasements like "perish the thought..."

'She has attracted admirers who have occasionally hung about the place. That is the only drawback which we have found to her, but we believe her to be a thoroughly good girl in every way.

'So much for the servants,' said Holmes. 'But what about the family itself?'

'I am a widower, and have an only son, Arthur. He has been a disappointment to me, Mister Holmes, a grievous disappointment. I have no doubt that I am myself to blame. People tell me that I have spoiled him. Very likely I have. When my dear wife died I felt that he was all I had dear to love. I could not bear to see the smile fade even for a moment from his face. I have never denied him a wish. Perhaps it would have been better for both of us had I been sterner, but I meant it for the best.

'It was naturally my intention that he should succeed me in my business, but he was not of a business turn. He was wild, wayward, and, to speak the truth, I could not trust him in the handling of large sums of money. When he was young he became a member of an aristocratic club, and there, having charming manners, he was soon intimate of a number of men with long purses and expensive habits. He learned to play heavily at cards and to squander money on the turf, until he had again and again to come and see me and implore me to give him an advance upon his allowance, that he might settle his debts of honour. He tried more than once to break away from the dangerous company which he was keeping, but each time the influence of his closest friend, Gaylon Schwinger, was enough to draw him back again.'

Sherlock Holmes rolled his eyes upwards to the gods. 'Would that be the unscrupulous cad and baronet, Schwinger with a 'c'?

'Indeed. I could not wonder that such a man as Sir Gaylon with a 'c' should gain an influence over him, for he has frequently brought him to my house, and I have found myself that I could hardly resist the fascination of his manner. He is older than Arthur, a man of the world to his fingertips, one who has been everywhere, and seen everything, a brilliant talker, everybody's friend, and a man of great personal beauty and I found him extremely attractive.'

Suddenly the air hung in the room like an ancient tapestry. He may not have been in the habit of molesting his maids and now we understood why. I found myself studying my fingers in detail, for no particular reason. I glanced over to Holmes, who raised his brows and shifted his weight around awkwardly. The banker studied us and, once again, read our minds.

'NO! No, no, no gentlemen! I merely meant that I found him attractive *as a character*. What is it about this neighbourhood? First, I am called a pimp. Then, I am accused of bedding my female staff. And now I am labelled homosexual. This is preposterous!' He nodded his head up and down and side-to-side. He was very upset. 'In fact, if you would let me finish, I was about to tell you that Sir Gaylon should be deeply distrusted. Far away from the glamour of his presence, I am convinced by his cynical speech and the look which I have caught in his eyes. So I think, and so, too, thinks my little Mary, who has a quick woman's insight into character.'

'His name and character are familiar to me as a bounder,' said Holmes. 'He thinks a lot of himself but without substance. Women mistrust him too. He is an abuser of the fairer sex.'

'As a banker, Mister Holmes, I can assure you that I have had to measure many chancers like Schwinger. Now, let me describe Mary. She is my niece, but when my brother died five years ago and left her alone in the world I adopted her and have looked upon her ever since as my daughter. She is a sunbeam in my house – sweet, loving, beautiful, a wonderful manager and housekeeper, yet as tender and quiet and gentle as a woman could be. She is my right hand. I do not know what I would do without her. In only one matter has she ever gone against my wishes. Twice my boy has asked her to marry him, for he loves her devotedly, but each time she has refused him. I think that if anyone could have drawn him into the right path it would have been she, and that his marriage might have changed his whole life; but now, alas, it is too late – for ever, too late!'

'Excuse me, gentlemen,' said I, 'but I assume that I would recognise a coronet if it came my way but who is this, or what is this Beryl?'

Sherlock Holmes and Mr. Holdup turned to face me, our guest nodding his head up and down with a look of extreme weariness at my enquiry. Just why was he nodding like? And keep doing it? The great detective flicked his long white fingers in the direction of the Palladian bookcase. 'You will find what you are looking for, Watson, in the seminary volume of all gemstones entitled *Guess's Carats & Facets* by the eminent Kingston-upon-Thames gemologist.'

Whilst I stood up and went in search of the said seminary volume, "Noddy" continued with his story.

'Imagine, Mister Holmes, that we had finished dinner that night. We were taking coffee in the drawing-room. I told Arthur and Mary my experience, and of the precious treasure which we had under our roof, suppressing only the name of my client.'

'Who is, I believe...' interjected Holmes, 'The Duke of Barrymore; The Margrave of Münsterland; The Earl of Felching; Le Duc de la Plage-Nu, Il Visconti di Del Monte and, most suitably, the Sultan of Beryl.'

My ears pricked up. 'The world's most internationally-renowned aristocrat? Surely not?'

'Keep searching, Watson...' mumbled Holmes.

I returned to my scouring of the rows of spines.

'You have guessed correctly, Mister Holmes,' sighed Mr. Noddy, his shoulders drooping in resignation. Goodness me, he was nodding his head again! 'When I am seated with the world's most internationally-renowned detective, should I be surprised?'

'Indeed not,' I remarked, reaching up and levering Mr. Guess's tome from its home. I started to flick through its pages.

'Dukes and earls wear coronets,' said he, 'and monarchs wear crowns, so the clue to his identity was in the style of the corona, Mister Holdup. Was anybody else in the drawing-room aside from you, your son and your niece?'

'Lucy Parr, who had brought in the coffee, had, I am sure, left the room; but I cannot swear that the door was closed. Mary and Arthur were much interested, and wished to see the famous coronet, but I thought it better not to disturb it.'

'"Where have you put it,"' asked Arthur.

'"In my own bureau."'

'"When you could have left it in the bank?"'

I nodded in appreciation of his son's perspicacity; this chap Arthur recognised as well as I his father's low level of common sense and high octane of stupidity. I had been leafing through the book and my eyes settled upon the chapter devoted to the qualities of a beryl. It was a valuable stone, mined all over the world, found in a myriad of carbon allotropes, which included emeralds and aquamarines. Very pretty, I am sure, but, dear adventure-enthusiast, they were hardly diamonds, were they? I sat back down on the Savonarola.

'"Well, I hope to goodness the house won't be burgled during the night,"' said he.

'"It is locked up,"' I answered.

'"Oh, and any old key will fit that bureau. When I was a youngster I have opened it myself with a key of the box room cupboard."'

'He often had a wild way of talking, so that I thought little of what he said. He followed me to my room, however, that night with a very grave face.

'"Look here, Dad," said he, with his eyes cast down. "Can you let me have two hundred pounds?"'

'"No, I cannot!" I answered sharply. "That is preposterous! I have been far too generous with you in money matters."'

'"You have been very kind," said he; "but I must have this money, or else I can never show my face inside the club again."'

'"And a very good thing, too!"' I cried.

'"Yes, but you would not have me leave it a dishonoured man," said he. "I could not bear the disgrace. I must raise the money in some way, and if you will not let me have it, then I must try other means."'

'I was very angry, for this was the third demand during the month. "You shall not have a farthing from me," I said, "and that's the end of it." He bowed and left the room without another word.'

'When he was gone I unlocked the bureau, made sure that my treasure was safe, and locked it again.

Then I started to go around the house to see that all was secure – a duty which I usually leave for Mary, but which I thought it well to perform myself that night. As I came down the stairs I saw Mary herself at the side window of the hall, which she closed and fastened as I approached.'

'"Tell me, Dad," said she, looking, I thought, a little unsettled and disturbed, "did you give Lucy, the maid, leave to go out tonight?"'

'"Certainly not."'

'"She came in just now by the back door. I have no doubt that she has only been to the side gate to see someone, but I think that it is hardly safe, and should be stopped."'

'"You must speak to her in the morning, or I will, if you prefer it. And are you sure that everything is fastened?"'

'"Quite sure, Dad."'

'"Then, goodnight."' I kissed her, and went to my bedroom, where I was soon asleep.

'I am endeavouring to tell you everything, Mister Holmes,' said he, nodding, 'which may have any bearing upon the case, but I beg that you will question me upon any point which I do not make clear.'

'On the contrary, your statement is singularly lucid.'

'I come to a part of my story now in which I should be particularly so. I am not a very heavy sleeper, and the anxiety in my mind tended, no doubt, to make me even less so than usual. About two in the morning, then, I was awakened by some sound in the house. It had ceased when I was awake, but it had left an impression behind it, as though a window had gently closed somewhere. I lay listening, with all of my ears. Suddenly, to my horror, there was a distinct sound of footsteps moving softly in the next room, I slipped out of bed, all palpitating with fear, and peeped around the corner of my dressing-room door.'

'"Arthur!" I screamed, "you villain! You thief! How dare you touch that coronet!"'

'The gas was half up, as I had left it, and my unhappy boy, dressed only in his shirt and trousers, was standing beside the light, holding the coronet in his hands. He appeared to be wrenching at it or bending it with all his strength. At my cry he dropped it from his grasp and turned as pale as death. I snatched it up and examined it. One of the gold corners, with three beryls in it, was missing.'

'"You blackguard!" I shouted, beside myself with rage. 'You have destroyed it! You have dishonoured me for ever! Where are the jewels you have stolen?"'

'"Stolen?"' he cried.

'"Yes, you thief!"' I roared, shaking him by the shoulder.

'"There are none missing. There cannot be any missing,"' said he.

'"There are three missing. And you know where they are. Must I call you a liar as well as a thief? Did I not see you trying to tear off another piece?"'

'"You have called me names enough," said he; "I will not stand it any longer. I shall not say another word about this business since you have chosen to insult me. I will leave your house in the morning and make my own way in the world."'

'"You shall leave it in the hands of the police!" I cried, half mad with grief and rage. "I shall have this matter probed to the bottom."'

'"You shall learn nothing from me," said he, with a passion such as I should not have thought was in his nature. "If you choose to call the police, let them find what they can."'

'By this time the whole house was astir, for I had raised my voice in my anger. Mary was the first to rush into my room, and at the sight of the coronet and of Arthur's face, she read the whole story in an instant, and, with a scream, fell down senseless to the ground. I sent the housemaid for the police and put the investigation into their hands at once.'

He nodded like mad. Holmes and I smiled at each other – not at Mr. Noddy's nodding but at the revelation of his call for the coppers. How many times had we heard a client announce this desperate decision as the final act in a matter of grief?

'When the inspector and a constable entered the house, Arthur, who had stood sullenly with his arms folded, asked me whether it was his intention to charge him with theft. I answered that it had ceased to be a private matter, but had become a public one, since the ruined crown was a national property.'

'Surely a National Treasure?' quipped I, 'with a capital N and a capital T?'

'Shut up, Watson!'

'Is he always this tiresome, Mister Holmes?'

'No. He chirrups like a canary only when he has ferouked all night, as he did last night. Pray, continue with your story.'

'I was determined that the law should have its way in everything. "At least," said Arthur, "you will not have me arrested at once. It would be to your advantage as well as mine if I might leave the house for five minutes."'

'"That you may get away, or perhaps that you may conceal what you have stolen?"' said I. 'And then realising the dreadful position in which I was placed, I implored him to remember that not only my honour, but that of one who was far greater than I, was at stake; and that he threatened to raise a scandal which would convulse the nation. He might avert it all if he would tell me what he had done with the three missing stones.'

'"You may as well face the matter," said I; "you have been caught in the act, and no confession would make your guilt more heinous. If you but make such reparation as is your power, by telling us where the beryls are, all shall be forgiven and forgotten."'

"Keep your forgiveness for those who ask for it," he answered, turning away from me with a sneer. I saw that he was too hardened for any words of mine to influence him. There was but one way for it. I called in the inspector and gave him into custody. A search was made at once, not only of his person, but of his room, and of every portion of the house where he could possibly have hidden the gems; but no trace of them could be found, nor would the wretched boy open his mouth for all our persuasions and our threats. This morning he was removed to a cell, and I, after going through all the police formalities, have hurried round to you, to implore you to use your skill in unravelling the matter. The police have openly confessed that they can at present make nothing of it. I have already offered a reward of a thousand pounds.' He nodded again; this time quite slowly and sagely.

A client with money! We should have him stuffed... This banker chap was about to be my payer of the rent and the salvation of my dignity. I warmed to him.

'When we worked for the King of Bohemia,' said I, with Holmes frowning deeply at me. 'We were given expenses on account.'

Holmes pursed his lips in extreme irritation. 'It was a mere gesture by a monarch.'

'No, no, Holmes, it was more than a gesture.' My goodness, I needed that rent money! 'Now let me think...' mused I, hand on chin, leaning back (for dramatic effect) in my chair and nearly falling off the ruddy thing because a Savonarola has no rails or splats. 'It was about seven hundred in cash and a bag of gold coins, and quite a large bag at that ...'

Holmes was fuming at me. He went puce in the face.

Mr. Holdup put up his hands to indicate I be silent. He leaned forward in his chair, his head nodding up and down like a pulse hammer, wishing to emphasise the gravity of his next enunciation. 'Gentlemen, I am a very wealthy man. You may go to *any* expense which you think necessary. No explanation will be required of *any* sum demanded. *Any* amount of money you wish to nominate or request will be delivered to you without question or inquiry.'

Suddenly the door crashed open, and there was Mrs. Hudson pushing her new keep-warm trolley, Sorrento, into the room. She must have been eavesdropping to arrive just as Mr. Noddy announced the grand opening of his wallet! She came to a halt at the mahogany and stood with her hands on her hips. She was staring at Mr. Holdup. I followed her eye-line and he was a sight to behold. Now the stupid banker had placed his hands on either side of his head and was rocking himself to and fro, droning to himself like a spoiled child whose grief has gone beyond words.

'My God, Mister Holmes, what shall I do?!' he whimpered, 'I have lost my honour! I have lost my gems! I have lost my son! And your housekeeper is convinced that I am a pimp! Oh what shall I do?'

I was thinking... do the decent thing, that's what you should do, and my eyes travelled over to the desk where I kept the Manstopper. Maybe if I was to offer him the Henry Holland revolver he would put an end to it all? But then I had a feeling I was being watched, and when I dashed my peepers over to Sherlock Holmes he was looking straight at me, whilst also waving his long, white index finger to put a stop to my wicked thoughts (but wearing the broadest grin you have ever seen)! We were in mental harmony about the necessity of this client, both for his unusual problem and his cash.

Mrs. Hudson assumed that Mr. Holdup had gone mad and laid up the breakfast. I turned my attention back to the rueful figure of our client, who, once again, was mopping his brow with his hanky.

'I merely meant, Mister Holdup,' said I, 'that we are looking for every detail to be revealed to us, so that we may investigate efficiently and thus not waste any of the monies or gold that you are about to leave with us on account of our expenses.'

'Money? You want money from me now? I never carry the stuff with me. It is left at my home, or in my office at the Bank. Does this mean that I should abandon this investigation with you?'

Mrs. Hudson squeaked like a mouse! Mr. Holdup swung his head round to look at her but it was Sherlock Holmes who started, as if a bolt of electricity had wound through him.

'Your case is of the highest fascination to me, Mister Holdup,' said Holmes. 'Money? What is money in a situation such as this? I have started upon it already, regardless of recompense.'

And before I could say: "absolutely essential" the great detective continued.

'The good Doctor raises a point when he asks if there is anything more to reveal before we accompany you to the scene of the crime. I would like, for instance, to know more about Mary. Does she go out much in Society?'

'No. She stays at home with me. We neither of us care for it.'

'That is unusual in a young girl.'

'She is of an opinionated nature. *Highly* opinionated. Besides, she is not so very young. She is four-and-twenty.'

'As in four-and-twenty blackbirds, baked in a pie?' quipped I, referring to the old English nursery rhyme, *Sing A Song of Sixpence*.

'No, sir! She is not black, sir! No! Nothing could be further from the truth!' said he, nodding furiously.

Confusion reigned! As luck would have it, Mrs. Hudson announced that breakfast was served. We moved over to the table and made ourselves comfortable whilst we watched her lift the silver covers off the plates. There was a small feast laid before us of eggs, bacon, sausages, tomatoes and kedgeree. Once she had poured the coffee Sherlock Holmes resumed his interrogation.

'This matter seems to have been a shock to Mary?' enquired he, flicking a porker onto his plate.

'Terrible! She is even more affected than I.' said Mr. Noddy slipping three of the five fried eggs onto his plate, the greedy pig, and placing a sausage in the middle.

'You have neither of you any doubt as to your son's guilt?' enquired the great detective, spooning the lion's and lionesses share of the kedgeree onto his plate and lobbing an egg on top of it.

'How can we have, when I saw him with my own eyes with the coronet in his hands?' whined the banker, now aiming a spoon at the tomatoes. I leaned in and dashed my fork forwards to stab one of them, with a cry of 'gangway!' to ensure unhindered passage but, alas, that didn't work. The greedy banker jousted my spoon aside and scooped up the whole plate of red fruit.

'I hardly consider that conclusive proof,' judged Holmes, now laying down some bacon in front of him with tongs and holding them high and out of my reach. 'Was the remainder of the coronet at all injured?'

'Yes, it was twisted.'

I grabbed the one egg that was left and whisked it over to my plate. In my haste, I broke its fragile surface. I gazed at the yolk as it spilled out its yellow life blood over the porcelain.

'Do you think, then, that he might have been trying to straighten it?' piped my companion, now waving the tongs in the air inquisitively. Now was my chance to spear a rasher or two!

'God bless you!' gasped the nodding banker, but not in reply to Sherlock Holmes's beautiful interpretation of Holdup's wayward son's actions but taking the waving tongs as an invitation to help himself to the bacon. 'You are doing what you can for him and for me...' said he, as he lunged into the pig belly with both fork and a knife and snaffled the lot. 'But it is too heavy a task. What was he doing there at all? If his purpose were innocent, why did he not say so?'

In total exasperation and no doubt some tiredness from the night before, I threw my knife and fork down onto the plate. What was the point in trying when I couldn't get into the trough? Holmes noticed and flicked his eyes at me. 'Shut up, Watson!' mumbled he, mid-mastication and then looked back at our new client. 'Precisely. And if he were guilty, why did he not invent a lie? His silence appears to cut both ways. There are several singular points about the case. What did the police think of the noise which awoke you for from your sleep?'

'They considered that it might be caused by Arthur's closing his bedroom door,' splurged Mr. Holdup through a mouth full of my breakfast.

'A likely story! As if a man bent on felony would slam the door so as to awake a household. What did they say, then, of the disappearance of these gems?' Holmes polished off his first sausage.

'They are still sounding the planking and probing the furniture in the hope of finding them. Mmm! This bacon is better than I get at Rothschild's!'

'Have they thought of looking outside the house?' said Holmes, now keen and intense, and flicking his fork toward the window with a tridented sausage. Now was my chance! I leaped up and swiped the porker off the prongs. I threw it into my mouth, all in one. Holmes glared as me for a second but then reverted to his new client.

'Yes, they have shown extraordinary energy. The whole garden has already been minutely examined.'

'Now, my dear sir,' said Holmes, placing his cutlery neatly upon a clean plate and leaning back in his chair, 'is it not obvious to you now, that this matter really strikes very much deeper than either you or the police were at first inclined to think? It appears to you to be a simple case; to me it seems exceedingly complex. Consider what is involved by your theory. You suppose that your son came down from his bed, went, at great risk, to your dressing-room, opened your bureau, took out the coronet, broke off by main force a small portion of it, went off to some other place, concealed three gems out of thirty-nine, with such skill that nobody can find them, and then returned with the other thirty-six into the room in which he exposed himself to the greatest danger of being discovered. I ask you now, is such a theory tenable?'

'But what other is there?' cried the highly-bearded banker, with a gesture of despair, and throwing his napkin onto his empty plate. 'If his motives were innocent, why does he not explain them?'

'It is our task to find that out,' replied Holmes, now standing up. 'So now, if you please, Mister Holdup, we shall set off for Streatham together and devote an hour to glancing a little more closely into details.'

The merchant banker stood up smartly, to attention.

'That's what I wanted to hear, Mister Holmes! Let us go forth at once!'

'Wait a moment...' I commanded.

'Watson, you are invaluable, but what are we waiting for?'

'For the payment of expenses yet to be incurred,' interrupted Mrs. Hudson. 'And that means you, sir, right at this moment, before your departure.'

Sherlock Holmes was shocked, sent reeling into speechlessness by our landlady's intrusion. In fact, this was not the case.

'But as I remarked earlier, Madam, sadly, I carry no cash.'

'A cheque will do.'

Wearing a rather piqued expression Mr. Holdup pulled out a garishly large cheque book and dashed off the necessary. He tore out the promissory note but then pondered a moment before scribbling a few words upon the obverse. He flicked it in the air with gay abandon and I wondered what he had written as it fluttered towards the centre of the table.

'There you are, madame...' said he, dismissively. He took off with Holmes towards the door. I watched the flight path of the cheque and, would you believe it? It landed smack bang in the middle of my broken egg!

I never had the chance to pick it out and read the message before there was a "for Pete's sakes, do come along, Watson!" from Holmes. I cursed my companion's impatience and set off after him.

* * *

We hailed a four-wheeler for our journey. When we set off all three of us were quiet. Maybe we had had long enough in the conversation pit already that morning. Each one of us had excuses for feeling frazzled. My curiosity was deeply stirred by the story to which we had listened, but I could not feel any sympathy for Noddy Holdup. What an idiot! How stupid had he been to take the Duke's coronet home with him to Streatham when he could have left it in his vault in the City? Not only would his bank have a proper safe but probably had guards as well; and, if events had turned out for the worst, it was likely to have its contents under insurance. How brainless could this banker be? Still, when one thought about the childishly simple methodology of his occupation – take money on deposit and pay a little interest and then lend it to someone else at ten times the rate – maybe I could comprehend why he thought the single-mortice lock in the bureau was the finest security. I confess that the guilt of the banker's son appeared to me to be as it did to his unhappy father, but still I had such faith in Holmes's judgment that I felt there must be some grounds for hope (as long as he was dissatisfied with the accepted explanation). Sherlock Holmes hardly spoke a word throughout the journey. He sat with his chin upon his breast, and his hat drawn over his eyes, sunk in the deepest thought. Our client appeared to have taken fresh heart at the little glimpse of hope which had been

Mr Holdup turned goldfish when he read the note from Mrs Hudson!

presented to him, and he even broke into a desultory chat with me over his business affairs. How boring was that? But when we made a short railway journey from Waterloo to Streatham he pricked my curiosity by taking a folded note from his pocket, opening it up and being immediately surprised by what he read. He then smiled contentedly at the conclusion he drew from it. In fact, Mr. Holdup's smile was long-lasting – all the way to Streatham railway station – so it must have been something other than money.

We made a short walk to arrive at Fairbank. I thought it was a rather modest residence for a financier of such great reputation. It was good-sized square house of white stone, standing back a little from the road. A double-carriage sweep, with a snow-clad lawn, stretched down in front to the two large iron gates which closed the entrance. On the right side was a small wooden wicket which led into a narrow path between two neat hedges stretching from the road to the kitchen door and forming the tradesman's entrance. On the left ran a lane which led to the stables and was not in itself within the grounds at all, being a public, though little used, thoroughfare. Holmes left us standing at the door, and walked slowly all around the house, across the front, down the tradesman's path, and so round by the garden behind and into the stable lane. He was studying the snow-covered ground intently. Mr. Holdup and I became bored of waiting. We went into the dining-room and waited by the fire until he should return. Whilst we were sitting there, the door opened, and a young lady came in. She was rather above the middle height, slim, with dark hair and eyes, which seemed darker against the absolute pallor of her skin. I wouldn't say that she was ugly but was not very attractive to men, with a sour face, like a dented bucket. To cap it all, her eyes were flushed with crying, which made her eye make-up smudge. I have to say, though, there was a plus side. She seemed to have a fabulous figure, as much as the cut of her dress afforded me a gentleman's insight. I could make out an ample top hamper. A most shapely eggtimer abdomen and finished off with a fine pair of long legs. Hmm, quite a package! But as she swept silently into the room she impressed me with a greater sense of her grief than the banker had done in the morning, and it was more striking in her as she was evidently a woman of strong character, with immense capacity for self-restraint. Disregarding my presence, she went straight to her uncle, and passed her hand over his head with a sweet womanly caress. As she bent over him I was afforded an eyeful of her peachy, which was her greatest asset; a truly beautiful sight, and...

'HOY!' she shouted suddenly, in an accent of estuary origination whilst standing up and swivelling on her heel to face me. 'Get your eyeball off of my arse!'

'No, no, dear lady! You don't realise...'

'STOP IT!' she yelled, jabbing her finger at me.

Before I could dampen her spirits she had turned back around to her uncle. Well, I thought, that was very kind of her to give me another eyeful of her *derrière*. I felt a serious twinge in the trouser department!

'You have given orders that Arthur should be freed, aint'chya, dad?' she asked him.

'No, no my girl, the matter must be probed to the bottom.'

She was still bending over. I was thinking the same way too.

'But I am so sure that he is innocent,' said she, pointing a forefinger at her left tit. 'You know what women's instincts are. I know he has done no harm. You'll be sorry for having acted so harshly.'

'I actually saw him with the coronet in his hands.'

'Oh, dad, really? He had only picked it up to look at it. Just take my word for it that he is innocent and let the matter drop.'

'I shall never let it drop until the gems are found. Never, Mary! Your affection for Arthur blinds you as to the awful consequences to me. Far from hushing the thing up, I have brought a gentleman down from London to inquire more deeply into it.'

She pointed at me again, her blues eyes blazing.

'What... HIM?!' she shouted incredulously. 'HIM?! All HE he's done since I walked into the room is eye me up!'

'He is not that gentleman I refer to. It is his friend.'

'GENTLEMAN?'

I stood up and shuffled around, looking all affable. 'Please, Miss, I was merely concerned about your pallid appearance.' I looked her in the eye. 'It is my professional opinion that you were, or you are, suffering from anaemia.'

'A professional arse-starer, that's what you are!' she cried.

'Please, miss, let me introduce myself. I am John Watson, a doc ...'

The front door banged open Sherlock Holmes walked into the house. His sudden appearance stopped me but not, unfortunately, Miss Mary.

'Dog? Yes, I know you are!' shouted Miss Mary, unabated. 'It is dogs like you that demean womanhood! Rubbing your eyeballs all over our bodies, your hands like tentacles, fantasising about how you would have your wicked way with us! Now, let me tell you...'

Goodness me, I had never been so grateful to see Holmes!

'I have made a thorough reconnaissance of the stable lane,' remarked he, standing on the mat knocking the snow from his shoes with a bemused smile upon his face as I was being harangued to death by this harpy. He raised his head to look at me and cracked a smile.

'Why? What for?' cried Miss Mary Holdup. 'What can you hope to find there?'

Holmes looked surprised by her outburst and decided not to rise.

'Holmes – may I introduce you to Miss Mary, Mister Holdup's niece.' Holmes nodded his head at her.

'This, Miss, is the ever-so famous detective, Mister Sherlock Holmes.'

'Another pervert, I'll bet!' she snarled, and then she turned her guns on my companion. 'Your friend here, the dog, has had his eyes all over me, like I was covered in frog spawn!'

Holmes walked over to her, still smiling – he was miles ahead! – and she was taken aback. She had expected him to come to my defence, no doubt, and now she trembled with anger.

'Calm yourself, my dear!' soothed he.

Miss Mary boiled up into a frightful rage. Frankly, I thought she was going to explode!

'Watson has his peculiarities, but they only seem odd to the layman, or, in your case, the laywoman. He told you that he is a doctor, yes?'

'No, he hasn't.' She looked over at me, confused. 'A real proper one, and all that?'

I nodded. Her face dropped and her shoulders drooped down.

'I am sorry, doctor,' said she, 'I am not myself right now, what with this horrible business and all that. I get carried away. I have to stand up for myself.'

'But he is still a dog' said Holmes suavolently. 'After he hoofed down all of the breakfast this morning.'

'I beg your pardon!'

'Ha!' Sherlock Holmes laughed at me in a certain way. So, he had made sure that I went hungry at breakfast this morning. Hmm! I would get my revenge later. I kept my peace for now, for I knew that when my companion was in such an ebullient mood that he had the measure of the mystery. He had either cracked the case or was slither of a slice away from it. He gave me a wink and settled himself into a chair near the fire. He rubbed his hands together.

'Now, Miss Holdup, might I ask you a question or two?'

She nodded meekly.

'You heard nothing yourself last night?'

'Nothing, until my uncle here began to speak loudly. When I heard that, I came down.'

'You shut up the windows and the doors the night before. Did you fasten all the windows?'

'Yeah., 'course I did'

'Were they fastened this morning?'

'Yeah, course they were.'

'You have a maid who has a sweetheart? I think that you remarked to your uncle last night that she had been out to see him?'

'Yeah, she done that.'

Miss Mary's eyes narrowed as her tide of anger rose again. 'She was the one with big ears! The one that waited in the drawing-room. The one that may have heard uncle's remarks about the coronet.'

'I see. You infer that she may have gone out to tell her sweetheart, and that the two may have planned the robbery.'

'What is the good use of all these vague theories?' cried Mr. Holdup impatiently. 'I have told you already that I saw Arthur with the coronet in his hands. It is preposterous, sir!'

'Wait a little, Mister Holdup. We must come back to that. About this girl, Miss Holdup. You saw her return by the kitchen door, I presume?'

'Yeah. When I went to see if the door was shut up proper for the night I caught her slipping in. I saw her geezer, too, in the gloom.'

'Do you know him?'

'Oh, yeah. Francis Prosper, the greengrocer. He's our fruit 'n' veg man.'

'This Francis Prosper stood,' said Holmes, 'to the left of the door – that is to say, farther up the path than is necessary to reach the door.'

'Yeah. So?'

'And he is a man with a wooden leg.'

Something like fear sprang up in the young lady's expressive black eyes. 'How do you know that? Are you like some sort of magician?'

But Holmes didn't respond. She smiled, but there was no answering smile in Holmes's thin, eager face.

'Now I should be very glad now to go upstairs,' said he. 'Perhaps I had better take a look at the lower windows before I go up.'

He walked swiftly round from one to the other, pausing only at the large one which looked from the hall to the stable lane. This he opened and made a very careful examination of the sill with his powerful magnifying lens. 'Now we shall go upstairs,' said he, at last.

All of us tramped up the unremarkable wooden staircase. The banker's dressing room was a plainly furnished little chamber with a grey carpet, a large bureau, and a long mirror. Holmes went to the bureau first and looked hard at the lock.

'Which key was used to open it?' he asked.

'That which my son himself indicated – that of the cupboard of the lumber-room.'

'Have you it here?'

'That is it on the dressing-table.'

Sherlock Holmes took it up and opened the bureau.

'It is a noiseless lock,' said he. 'It is no wonder that it did not wake you. This case, I presume, contains the coronet. We must have a look at it.' He opened the case, and, taking out the diadem, he laid it upon the table. It was a magnificent specimen of the jeweller's art, and the thirty-six stones were the finest and shiniest that I had ever seen. At one side of the coronet was a crooked cracked edge, where a corner holding the three gems had been torn away.

'Now see here, Mister Holdup,' said Holmes. 'Here is the corner which corresponds to that which has been so unfortunately lost. Might I beg that you will break it off.'

The banker recoiled in horror. 'I should not dream of trying!' said he in astonishment.

'Then I will.' Holmes suddenly forced his strength upon it, but without result. 'I feel it give a little,' said he; 'but, though I am exceptionally strong in the fingers, it would take me all my time to break it.'

'I say, Holmes, may I give it a try?' said I.

The great detective handed me the diadem.

'An extraordinarily strong strongman from the local circus could not do it, let alone a soft-fingered physician like you, Watson.'

'Oh, ha, ha, Holmes. I suggest you watch me very closely...'

'I do. Always.'

'I shall have you know that I know more than most about the black art of bending metals. It is all thanks to Yogi Bogi, my batman in Kabul.'

'But you had told that your batman was Herman-the-German?'*

'Him, too. But once the regiment had been posted to Afghanistan all of us officers had been assigned native servants as well. Mine was Yogi Bogi, who had acquired the rare and delicate ability to make metals

---

* see *The Mysterious Marriage of the Gay Bachelor*

more malleable by finger telepathy, the sheer force of natural brain waves.'

Miss Holdup burst into laughter, the cheeky chit! At least Holmes was more polite – he gave a stifled yawn of disbelief – and, predictably, the banker slapped his knee and shouted 'Preposterous!'

'Oh, Mister Holdup, I can tell you, hand on heart, that it is true. Yogi Bogi spent many hours entertaining us in the officers' mess by bending spoons and forks and knives into knots and clusters and loops using only the lightest touch of his finger and thumb. Now, what do you say to me performing the same to this unblemished corner of the coronet?'

'If you were to be successful, Doctor,' said he, nodding with menace and going red in the face, 'I would not go into just an uncontrollable temper, I WOULD GO BERSERK!'

'Cast your fears overboard, sir,' said Holmes, placatingly, almost laughing, 'and moor your anxiety by the dockside. This Yogi servant may have been a fakir who destroyed large swathes of the regimental cutlery, but I can assure you, that Doctor Watson is no fakir himself.'

'Oh, if you say so, Mister Holmes... Do as you will, Doctor.'

Permission granted, I sat down upon a well-positioned chair. I laid my right hand upon the opposite corner of the coronet from that which was already missing. I closed my eyes so that I may focus my concentration without distraction and drained all of the power from my brain down my arms, into my hands and through my index finger and thumb onto the gold structure. Would the precious metal soften, just like it did so often for Yogi in the officers' mess all those years ago? I drifted off into a trance – just as Yogi taught me – my vocal-chords vibrating and a tremolo drifting up from my diaphragm. Vaguely, in the distance, I could hear Holmes continuing his investigation…

'Don't mind him, Mister Holdup – he hasn't got a clue what he's doing. Now, to return to last night… If the corner had been broken off the diadem right here, there would have been a noise like a pistol shot, yes? So, do you tell me that all this happened within a few yards of your bed, and that you heard nothing at all?'

'Nothing, but I do not know what to think. It is all dark to me.'

'But perhaps it may grow lighter as we go.' Holmes turned his attention to the niece. 'What do you think, Miss Holdup?'

'Huh! I am surrounded by men. Useless men! So, are you surprised when I say that I still share my uncle's perplexity in the same way as before your arrival? You shouldn't be!'

'Thank you, Miss, but I find that being a man never precludes a successful outcome for my clients.'

Miss Mary Holdup put on a face like a slapped child. Holmes turned to his client.

'Now, Mister Holdup, your son had no shoes or slippers on when you saw him?'

'Nothing! Just his trousers and shirt.'

'Thank you. We have certainly been favoured with extraordinary luck during this inquiry, and it will be entirely our own fault if I do not succeed in clearing the matter up. With your permission, Mister Holdup, I shall now continue my investigations outside.'

Holmes went out of the house alone. Mister Holdup had a call of nature, made his excuses and headed towards the lavatory, which left Miss Mary and I alone in the room. I continued to hold the corner strut of the diadem b'twixt thumb and forefinger, my left arm resting on arm of the chair. I caught her staring at me through flinty eyes, slitted deliberately to take in my moves whilst trying to meditate. Then, she smiled and walked over to me. Actually, she waltzed, with a fresh look in her eye, one that I hadn't seen before, which I can only describe as scarily Bohemian. This was a very different Miss Mary from the one I had seen before! She stopped, right next to me. I felt her hot breath blowing off my ear. I could feel her warmth. I could smell her aroma, and it wasn't just a French perfume. There was something animalistic in the air.

'I say, Watson!' she declared, trying to imitate Sherlock Holmes. 'I saw the way you looked me up. It wasn't as a doctor... it was as a man! As red-blooded-a-man as I have ever met. A man that is excited by the shape of a woman, like what I am...'

And with that appalling abuse of language, she grabbed my spare hand, pulled her blouse asunder and clamped me onto her breast. Oh, my goodness, she was so marvellously soft and beautiful! I kneaded her warm flesh with heavenly enthusiasm. She started to moan. My chant modulated to be in tune with hers. We were man, woman and beryl coronet in total harmony. But there was more! She dropped a hand down towards her hips. Her fingers delved under the waistline of her skirt, burrowing down until she arrived at what we know lies below... She crossed her eyes as her arm started to move rhythmically. She closed her eyes. She moaned louder and louder whilst uttering the words "I am woman..." over and over. A heady scent of musk on a hot summer's evening infused my olfactory; of nutty nutmeg and ripe bananas, the addictive aroma of arousal. My sap was rising! Her body gyrated into a rhythm, rubbing up against me. Her movement became more frenzied. I became more excited. Before long she was thrashing from side to side and it was all I could do to hold onto her. Eventually, she threw herself up rigid; she arched her back and shuddered, like a dog shaking the water off its coat. My goodness, she had reached a climax! And I must have joined her, the experience being so intense that I am not certain what happened to me, but suddenly I was holding the separated three-gemmed corner of the coronet in my hand! I gazed at it, absolutely amazed that an orgasm delivered me such super-human strength! I held it aloft.

'Oh, Yogi, you genius fakir!' I shouted out loud to the world.

A blood-curdling scream ripped through the room! It was a post-orgasmic Miss Holdup, who now had her hands clamped to her cheeks, jumping up and down screaming at me. Recognising the separated corner of the National Treasure she fell to the floor.

The front door slammed open in response to Miss Mary's shrill scream of alarm. There stood Sherlock Holmes, on-point, his feet heavy with snow and his features as inscrutable as ever.

'Oh, by Beelzebub, Watson, what have you done?' exclaimed Holmes in genuine surprise and then collapsing into laughter.

Then the hallway door slammed open, also in response to Miss Mary's shrill scream of alarm. There stood Mr. Holdup, a face full of inquisition, his trouser fly wide open and his manhood dangling out.

'Who? What?' Then he zeroed-in on my triumphal handful. His eyes bulged, like his stomach was a hot-air balloon being squeezed by a giant hand, and he nodded furiously.

'BUT WHY?!' he howled, his face as red as a turkey cock. He marched across the room, his head bowed with murderous intent. Then, he ran at me, his dickie-doodah wagging from side to side.

'YOU PREPOSTEROUS MONSTER!' he screeched.

What a frightening sight he was -- big and red and fuming with his *coq sportif* flaylling around in front of him like a corn thresher! I leapt out of my seat, jigged to one side and ran for the safety of a door. Luckily, Miss Mary stopped her uncle in his tracks and held on to him. He was struggling livid, all red-faced and angry, snorting like the town bull. He shouted: "You wait until I get my hands on you!" Soon, Sherlock Holmes was with me. He snatched the gilded jewellery from my hand and handed it to our client with a stern, no-nonsense accompaniment.

'Calm down, Mister Holdup! This further defacing of the diadem is irrelevant. Once I have recovered the section that is missing it will make little difference to the master jeweller who makes the repair.'

'But the missing gems, Mister Holmes. Where are they?'

'I cannot tell.'

The banker wrung his hands. 'I shall never see them again!' he cried.

"Holmes! It is a coronet of *premature emasculation!*"
"It certainly came off in your hand," said he.

'I shall return to my rooms. If you call upon me in Baker Street tomorrow morning between nine and ten I shall be happy to do what I can to make it clearer. I understand that you give me *carte blanche* to act for you, provided only that I get back the gems, and that you place no limit on the sum I may draw.'

'I would give my fortune to have them back.'

'Then it is farewell for now. And, by the way, it is just possible that I may have to come over here again before evening.'

'Don't bring HIM with you!' were the final words I heard as Holmes bustled me out of the room and into the lane outside.

* * *

We embarked upon our homeward journey via the same route and modes of transport, starting with Shanks's pony. It seemed to me that my companion's mind was made up about the case, although what his conclusions were was more than I could even dimly imagine. Several times I endeavoured to sound him out upon that point, but he always glided away to some other topic. I moved away from the subject and on to the prospect of the trimming down of Mr. Holdup's personal fortune via our fees if he could solve the case, such was the desperation of our stupid banker client. Once again, and as per usual when the conversation turned to money, Holmes ignored my entreaties with a wave of his long, white fingers. At last, I gave it over in despair – I was too famished for arguments.

It was not yet three o'clock when we found ourselves in our rooms once more, having stopped off at a telegraph office at Waterloo station. I was hungry and tired. I gave the bell-pull a tug in the hope of something to eat but there was no sound of movement from Mrs. Hudson downstairs. Sherlock Holmes had hurried off to his chamber and was now standing before me in a three-piece worsted of low quality. His hair was a mess and he clutched a tatty top hat. He gave the appearance of a mad professor, like he didn't know if he was coming or going; he was a perfect example of the upper echelons of *intelligencia* that crowned the cream of Society in this great country of ours.

'You are off to The Athenaeum, I suppose?' commented I, whilst leaning on the bell-pull for the third time.

'You are wrong, Doctor. I am to meet with Mycroft and must therefore grace the threshold of the Diogenes Club,' said he, very matter-of-fact. 'I only wish that you could come with me, Watson, but I fear that it won't do.'

'I have never been to the Diogenes and know very little about it, apart from the fact that it is a club where one person may not converse with another. I have never heard of anything quite so ridiculous.'

'It is quite "PREPOSTEROUS!"' shouted Holmes.

We fell about laughing. The singular pomposity of our client was eminently satirical and mutually appreciated.

'You are a natural chatterbox, Watson. You cannot imagine a space of non-communication such as the Diogenes. But let me inform you that there is a certain sense of bliss in that serene, soothing atmosphere of silence. And you are not quite correct in your criticism; there is one room at least where conversation is permitted.'

'Really? One room?' I have to tell you, dear adventure enthusiast, that made all the difference to me. Holmes sensed my change of mood.

'I warn you, Watson, that if you change your mind, you will be meeting a very dangerous man.'

'I am the correspondent on this case. I shall join you and I shall bring the Manstopper.'

'Dressed like that you would be left standing on the pavement outside. Go and find your oldest suit, Doctor. We need to make you look as disreputable and disrespectful as possible.'

'Oh, really, Holmes?'

'I mean it. I shall find you something to eat whilst you change. And don't forget that revolver.'

* * *

We resumed our adventure fifteen minutes later by riding in a Hansom towards Oxford Street. Holmes had taken the Manstopper off of me and somehow, goodness knows how, concealed the enormous weapon inside his suit jacket. Still, I didn't bother to think about it too much when I clapped my eyes upon the emergency scoff that he had made for me; it was a thick slice of cold sirloin placed crudely in between two rounds of bread to make a life-saver of a sandwich. I had been brought up to eat in private, behind closed doors and never in a public space, so I am embarrassed to confess that I tucked into it *en route* like a hungry dog. The crumbs fell down onto my suit and just as I attempted to brush them off, my companion stayed my hand. I tried again, and the long fingers of the great detective grabbed my wrist and shook his head. How very strange it all seemed.

It was not long before I found myself standing on an old stone doorstep of a house in St. James's, at the bottom of the hill, just behind the palace. This was the home of the Diogenes Club. Sherlock Holmes went to great pains to help me alight from the cab without losing too many crumbs from the cloth. A craggy old brontosaurus of a porter opened the door and cast his eye over the two of us; at the sight of the sandwich detritus, he raised his brows and nodded approval. He ushered us into the building and led us through the sparsely-decorated hallway. There was something very unusual about this place and as we walked through drawing rooms I cast a keen eye over men of various years dotted around the spaces as individuals, all of them reading journals or newspapers or books. Just like me and my companion, they were dressed in ill-fitting or shabby suits. Some sat in plain armchairs and others at writing desks, but it was accumulation of reading materials that was the most startling aspect of the club; instead of paintings and pictures on the walls there was shelving, with rows and rows of books and magazines crammed onto them. They were also piled up in stacks upon the floors – one room dedicated entirely to old newspapers – and there were even some scrolls. It was an emporium of clutter! But here the strangest thing of all: every room was dead quiet, apart from the occasional scratching of pen on paper.

We walked down a corridor at the rear of the building. When we reached the very last room the door was opened for us and the porter then disappeared. We walked into a rather splendid space. The walls were painted jet black and scumbled in gold leaf, finished in a high glaze varnish over the top that reflected the soft glows from exotic gas lighters. Paintings and artefacts of great curiosity were dotted around the space, and there were sumptuous sofas and settees to park one's posterior in comfort.

The only person in the room was Mycroft Holmes. He placed the pink papers he had been studying onto the table in front of him, pinched his nose and raised himself up from his seat. He was slightly taller than Sherlock and more thick-set. He bore the features of a personable man, and I would say that although it was rumoured that he shared Sherlock's exceptional level of intellect, it was his brother who had been blessed with the good looks.

'Welcome, gentlemen, to the Strangers Room. Ah! Doctor Watson. I perceive the detritus of the beef sandwich helped you to gain access to the club. After all, and no offence intended, it would not be our custom to admit grammar school *alumni*. Well done, Sherlock! That was a cunning addition.'

'It was a palpable prop for a simple distraction,' remarked my bosom friend. 'Just regard the suit.'

'Ah, yes, indeed. That, Doctor, is a remarkable visa. Even if its tightness causes you the briefest moments of discomfort it has been worth the experience. What I mean is, who would have thought that you had even walked past the George Willcox Grammar School wearing it, let alone attend that establishment as a pupil, which I believe you did, Doctor, for five years. You did? I suspect this item of sartorial elegance was a hand-you-down from your... godfather?'

'Yes, you are correct,' I confessed. 'From great uncle Harry.'

'Ah, that is satisfying,' retorted Mycroft, his face

grinning, waving a triumphant finger in the air. 'He had to be your uncle or your godfather.'

'Actually, I deduce that he was both,' remarked Holmes, with a smile when I nodded.

'Ah! And also, I believe, he was a performer in the theatre.'

I nodded again.

'Oh come, come, Mycroft, try harder! He was a dancer,' said Sherlock Holmes, barging in before I could reply.

'I never told you that!' I shouted, in awe.

'But Sherlock, did you know that he rolled his own cigarettes.'

'Oh yes, brother dear, that is obvious.'

'This is ridiculous!' I shouted.

'But you do realise, my dear brother, that he was left-handed?' declared Mycroft. 'Other than that, I believe we cannot deduce any more, would you not agree my dear Sherlock?'

I was standing in between the two most deductive minds in the country. I put up my hands in surrender and started to laugh.

'No, Mycroft, there is more. One only has to look at the wear on the hem of the turn-ups to deduce high-speed dancing was a favourite past-time of the owner. Then, there is slightly longer sleeves of the jacket, an allowance made by his tailor for lifting of the arms when performing, like so...'

Sherlock Holmes made a poor attempt at toes and scuffs, single and double, flexing his outstretched arms from the elbows.

'I see what you mean, Sherlock. He was, therefore, a tap-dancer,' slithered Mycroft, a marvellous serpentine smile spreading across his face.

'And just how did you deduce my great uncle was a left-handed tap-dancer?' I enquired.

'Oh, is he not a Godsend for you, Sherlock? He asks the questions that you would dearly like *me* to make! In answer to your question, Doctor: it is common knowledge amongst certain men of high education that a high a percentage of tap dancers are left-handed. Quite simply, I played the odds.' He leaned in closer to his brother. 'Really, Sherlock, if your theory depends entirely upon the wear and tear of a trouser leg to ascertain your deduction, I wouldn't pursue this style of detective work, if I was you.'

The great detective collapsed into laughter. He broke away from Mycroft, slapped his thigh hard and exclaimed: 'Ha! Nothing changes with you, Mycroft...' And when his brother started laughing along too I got the impression that this was an old routine. A knock at the door interrupted us all.

'Come!' barked Mycroft. The door swung open and there, standing in the portal, was one of the most self-satisfied creatures I have ever seen. He was terribly over-dressed in his immaculate morning coat, shimmering silk waistcoat and shiny brogues. He peacocked himself, so that we may take him in, as would a leading actor being saluted by his adoring public at *The Garrick*.

'Wotcha, mooshies!' he said, with a glaring grin of brilliant white gnashers and a flourish of his right hand.

'Ah, Sir Gaylon,' said Mycroft, invitingly. 'Thank you for joining us at such short notice.'

'My pleasure, matey,' said our visitor, all off-hand and casual, his pencil-thin moustache twitching like gossamer caught on a wavering wire. He swaggered into the room, as if he was the richest man in the world. In fact, the more I studied him, the more I thought of him as a cunning fox, padding his way down a forest path on his way to the unsuspecting hen-house, his eyes flicking from one person to the next, weighing us up individually before choosing his position with utmost precision to make himself the centre of attention.

The door closed loudly and we turned to see why. We looked around to see Sherlock Holmes with his hand on the doorknob and a look of restrained impassion upon his features. He, too, was weighing up the opposition.

'Steady on, chap,' quipped the baronet to Holmes, 'it's a door, you know, not a guillotine!'

He shook hands with Mycroft and took the opportunity to move in closer to him. 'Your telegram caught me just right, just after a spot of lunch with a client. What with all this snow lying about, the turf is out of action. I had nothing to do but park my posterior until the tables warmed up for the evening.' Sir Gaylon rubber his hands together furiously. 'Got to make up the shekels somewhere, eh matey?'

'I should explain,' declared Mycroft to his brother and I, 'Sir Gaylon is an accountant of the turf by day and a skilled player of the tables by evening. But where are my manners? May I introduce you... Sir Gaylon Schwinger, this is my brother, Mister Sherlock Holmes.'

'Have we not met before?' said Holmes, tersely.

'I've heard of you, matey. The amateur detective, eh?'

Sherlock Holmes's face darkened but he held his peace and retreated to the fireplace where he leaned against the mantelpiece.

'And this chap here is his assistant, Doctor Watson.'

'Your sidekick, Mister Holmes? The quack? Well, you're not a real doctor, are you? You just write about little meets like this and flog it to that glossy mag, eh?'

'You may need my "quack" medical skills sooner than you can imagine, Sir Gaylon.'

I delivered my line with sufficient menace to make the little greaser throw back his head and laugh himself red in the face. I took up Mycroft's offer of a rather uncomfortable chair, as did Sir Gaylon who squirmed into seat, muttering "what a pair!" just loud enough for us to hear him.

'I have to tell you, Mycroft...' said our visitor slyly, 'any time this jolly joint of yours wishes to buy some decent furniture, I am your man.' He tapped the side of his nose. 'Get my meaning, matey?' He gave up tapping and tried to sit up straight but squirmed. My (hopeful) diagnosis? Haemorrhoids.

'The Diogenes is a club that embraces the bare necessities required to sustain human life, so that the mind may ingest the writings of mankind most purely, and without distraction. The founding gentlemen of this club are inspired by the long-suffering Diogenes himself, the Roman philosopher who dedicated his life to thinking rather than eek a living of even meagre comfort. Therefore, the chairs and seats reflect his way of life.'

Sherlock Holmes interceded: 'However, I believe that Diogenes lived like a dog and slept in an empty wine barrel, which none of the members seem to do.'

'I said "inspired" not replicated, Sherlock.'

'Well, it don't matter a ha'peth to my arse, maties. It is still screaming sore!'

Such poor language was not received well. Mycroft sniffed the air. Sherlock rolled his eyes. I looked over to the mantelpiece and paid unusual attention to the marble bust of Diogenes himself and wondering to myself if Sir Gaylon had gone to Eton.

'A thinking-man's posture requires poise,' said our host, 'not comfort for relaxation.'

'Enough!' cried Sherlock Holmes. 'A boy lies in prison whilst we debate the merits of the best environment in which to induct information and philosophise. Sir Gaylon, would you like to tell me how long you have been in a relationship of non-marital unity with Miss Mary Holdup.'

'Mary? She has a face like a bag of spanners but wow! What a fabulous racing chassis, eh, boys?'

We raised our brows at this annoying observation but said nothing in reply.

'Haw, haw, haw,' chortled he, having to say something. 'Mister Sherlock Holmes, ever the angler!'

'But I am correct, am I not?'

'Maybe, but, my dear chap, her opinions seem to be strong and individual. She champions her gender's attributes most earnestly; thus, it is a hell of a job to have a relationship with a girl like that.'

'"Earnestly?!"' I cried out loud. 'According to Miss Holdup, I am a sex maniac!'

Sir Gaylon made an inquisitive raise of his brows and nodded. 'I have no idea what you are talking about, Doc. I have never met you before; you could be anything. Come to that, I hardly know the girl, let alone her opinions. Anything else, chaps?'

'You know her much better than you are making out,' said Holmes, wagging his forefinger at Sir Gaylon. 'You were her lover! How else would you recruit a confederate that resided in the house whose loyalty to her uncle was otherwise insurmountable?'

Sir Gaylon dropped the jaunty face.

Without warning, Holmes suddenly dashed towards Sir Gaylon and dipped down to lift his left foot by the ankle. He took a good look at the sole of his black leather boot. Sir Gaylon was taken by surprise, and he pulled his leg back, yanking the boot from Holmes's grasp, but the great detective had seen enough.

'What the devil do you think you are doing, sir?' he cried out whilst standing up.

Holmes retreated to the same position at the mantelpiece as he had been in before. Sir Gaylon returned to his seat.

'In the snow this morning there was a double line of tracks. One was a booted man with the left sole marked the same as yours, Sir Gaylon. And there was a second line which I saw with delight belonged to a man with naked feet. I was at once convinced from what I saw that the latter was Mr. Holdup's son, Arthur. The first had walked both ways, but the other had run swiftly, and, as his tread was marked in places over the depression of the boot, it was obvious that he had passed after the other. I followed them up and found that they led to the hall window. That was how you hoped to gain access to the house as your boots had worn away all the snow while waiting. Then I walked to the other end, which was a hundred yards or more down the lane. I saw where you had faced round, where the snow was cut up, as though there had been a struggle, and, finally, where a few drops of blood had fallen, to show me that I was not mistaken. You had then run down the lane, and another little smudge of blood showed that it was you who had been hurt. When you came to the high-road at the other end, I found that the pavement had been cleared, so there was an end to the clue.

As one fact after another spilled from the great detective's mouth Sir Gaylon's face darkened. I hoped that he would be able to control himself.

'On entering the house,' continued Sherlock Holmes, 'I examined the sill and the framework or the hall window with my lens, and I could at once see that someone had passed out. I could distinguish the outline of an instep where the wet foot had been placed when coming in. I was then beginning to be able to form an opinion as to what had occurred. A man had been waiting outside the window – that was you, Sir Gaylon – and someone had brought you the gems. The deed had been overseen by Arthur Holdup and he had pursued you. He struggled with you. You both tugged at the coronet, your united strength causing injuries which neither could have affected. Arthur had won the fight and returned with the prize but you, Sir Gaylon, had been left with a fragment in your grasp. The only remaining question to be answered was the identity of your accomplice who brought you the coronet in the first place, and there is only one answer to that. It was Miss Mary Holdup.'

'My word, Sherlock,' remarked Mycroft, pricking the air with his forefinger, 'that is a remarkable piece of deduction. Well done! But how can you be sure that this loyal niece could embarrass her uncle so?'

Sir Gaylon shifted uneasily in his chair, his posterior being less troubled now than his mind.

'It is an old maxim of mine that when you have excluded the impossible, whatever remains, however improbable, must be the truth. It could not have been Mister Holdup who brought the coronet down, so there only remained his niece and the maids. But if it were the maids, why should Arthur allow himself to be accused in their place? There could be no possible reason. As he loved his cousin, however, there was an excellent explanation why he should retain her secret – the more so as the secret was a disgraceful one. When I remembered that you had seen her at that window, and how she had fainted on seeing the coronet again, my conjecture became a certainty.'

Really, Mister Cleverclogs...' rasped Sir Gaylon, 'it is not a racing certainty. You have no proof.'

'But you have already confessed to being her lover, Sir Gaylon,' said I. 'How else could you know that Miss Holdup has to her benefit what you described as "a racing chassis?" This is a fact that I am in a position to confirm at first-hand, one hundred per cent.'

And I preened myself proudly as the penny dropped with every man in the room that I had been intimate with Miss Mary Holdup. So, whilst I held the stage for once in my life, I told them what had occurred that very morning. The onanism; the dual climax; everything. Sherlock Holmes's eyes bulged like a goldfish laying chickens' eggs, and Sir Gaylon swung his arms out wide, palms up, his jaw working up and down like a beached guppy.

'So, I deduce,' I finished off, 'that only the most intimate of a relationship between the two of you could have reaped such a poignant remark.'

'Sir Gaylon!' announced the great detective. 'You are undone. Give in!'

Sir Gaylon bared his teeth, his spittle foaming on his lips! He lost all self-control, leaping up from his seat and throwing himself at Sherlock Holmes whilst plunging his right hand into his inside coat pocket. I could see that he was trying to fish out a revolver. It snared in his pocket, which gave Sherlock Holmes just enough time to lunge forward two steps, grab him by the collar with one hand and clap the Manstopper to his head. Sir Gaylon went limp, threw up his hands and collapsed into easy laughter, as if he hadn't moved from his chair.

'Mister Holmes! You have the better of me,' said he, all affable. 'How may I help you?'

'I am in a position to offer you a decent price for the stones you hold,' said the great detective. 'One thousand pounds apiece.'

Sir Gaylon became even more reasonable and let his arms droop by his sides. 'Why, bugger it all, matey! I've let them go at six hundred for the three!'

Mycroft sighed and made a resigned wave of his hand in resignation. Sherlock Holmes looked over to me.

'Doctor, you will please find a pencil and some notepaper and take down the particulars of the receiver of the stolen gems which Sir Gaylon is about to impart to you.'

The manstopper was a boon at parties, bar mitzvahs and ugly encounters with small-time crooks.

The great detective withdrew the overweight handgun and placed it back inside his jacket.

"There will be no prosecution, Sir Gaylon,' said Mycroft, very matter-of-fact, 'if you cooperate with my brother. That I can promise you.'

'As I have that promise from the Chief Constable's secretary…' said he, flicking his eyes at Mycroft, 'you leave me no choice.'

So, Sherlock Holmes's brother was a policeman. Of sorts…

* * *

The next morning I went out to find the daily papers, the boy having failed to deliver *The Times* and our usual selection of local rags. I found one easily enough. It was when I was letting myself back in to 221B, that I had the minor shock of finding Mr. Holdup making his way up the stairs whilst Mrs. Hudson was leaning out of her apartment door. Strange? They both jumped when I opened the door, as if they had been caught in the middle of a something secretly illicit. Certainly, they had not expected me to find them in such a position. As Mr. Holdup and I climbed the wooden hill in silence, I reflected upon my return journey to 221B just now and certainly the grand financier had not been in view in any direction. I deduced that he had been leaving Mrs. Hudson's apartment. *Mighty* strange!

I guided our client towards the breakfast table and there was Sherlock Holmes with a cup of coffee in one hand and looking as fresh and trim as possible. When Mr. Holdup sat down in the armchair I provided for him, he slumped heavily into it. I was shocked to see the change which had come over him, for his face, which was naturally a broad and massive mould, was now pinched and fallen in, while his hair seemed to be at least a shade whiter.

'I do not know,' he said, 'what I have done to be so severely tried,' said he. 'Only two days ago I was a happy and prosperous man, without a care in the world. Now I am left to a lonely and dishonoured age. Our sorrow comes close upon the heels of another. My niece Mary has deserted me.'

Holmes and I glanced at one another, hardly surprised, but we didn't wish to reveal our prior knowledge that Sir Gaylon had left his mark upon her.

'Her bed was empty this morning and had not been slept in,' he wailed. 'Her room was empty, and a note lay for me upon the hall table. It said: "Mr Dearest Uncle – I feel that I have brought the trouble upon you, and that if I had acted differently this terrible misfortune might never have occurred. I cannot, with this thought in my mind, ever again be happy under your roof, and I feel that I must leave you forever. In life or in death, I am your loving... Mary." Why, oh why, Mister Holmes?'

'There has been an understanding of the licentious kind between Sir Gaylon Schwinger and your niece, Mary. They have now fled together.'

'My Mary? Licentious? Impossible!'

'It is, unfortunately, more than possible. It is certain. Neither you nor your son knew the true character of this man when you admitted him into your family circle. He is one of the most dangerous men in England – a ruined gambler; a turf snitch; an absolutely desperate villain; a man without heart or conscience...'

'And a second-hand woman dealer.'

'Oh, no!' wailed the merchant banker.

'Thank you, Watson, but that is enough. Mister Holdup, your niece knew nothing of such men. When he breathed his vows to her, as had done to a hundred before her, she flattered herself that she alone had touched his heart.'

Oh, dear, Holmes was miles off in his assessment of Miss Mary. She was hardly an innocent spinster but I hadn't been given the opportunity to tell him that she was a borderline nymphomaniac.

'The devil knows best what he said, but at last she became his tool, and was in the habit of meeting up with him nearly every evening.'

'For what purpose?''

'For carnal union.'

'No! Not my Mary! She is chaste. Sir, that is preposterous! I cannot, and I will not, believe it!' cried the banker, with an ashen face. 'Why would she do such a thing?'

'For the same reason that you spent the night downstairs here with Mrs. Hudson.'

Our client's jaw dropped six inches – well past the length of his beard.

'The reason that stretches back in the mists of time, Mister Holdup: that man, or woman, cannot live by food alone. Would you not agree, Doctor?'

So that was why Noddy Holdup and our landlady looked so sheepish in the hallway just now. Mrs. Hudson in a state of sexual entwinement with Mr. Holdup? I gawped at the banker for a reaction, but there was none. I switched my gaze to Holmes. He nodded. I turned back to the banker, who dropped his shoulders, which I took to be a confession.

'Well, it is no wonder that you look so tired this morning, Mister Holdup!' observed I.

'She is insatiable! I am half the man I was of yesterday evening when I arrived here in Baker Street. I am shredded! Absolutely shredded, but I feel so used!' said Mr. Holdup.

'Why would that be so?' said Holmes. 'Surely you have been blessed by the union of a man of your waning years and that of the youthful Mrs. Hudson, physiologically-speaking of course.'

'There was no such thing as a union, Mister Holmes. She is a dedicated fellationist.'

'Indeed?'

'Holmes, surely you have written a treatise on fellatilly?'

'I have, Watson, but philately is stamp collecting and hardly relevant.'

As I have indicated before, the great detective was under-educated in the ways of the flesh...

'All I can tell you, as a gentleman, sir, is that Mrs. Hudson is the most accomplished stamp collector that I have ever met! She is relentless, sir! But just when I was thinking to myself how truly blessed I was, then, Mister Holmes, this morning that illusion was shattered when she laid out some blueprints for the erection of a new commercial property on Oxford Street.' She asked me to lend her the money to pay for it!'

'Ha!' said Holmes, slapping his thigh, 'and she asked you to lend her money to pay for the erection! A more apposite word in this particular situation is not available in the lexicon!' He slapped his hand down again and threw his head back laughing.

'Oh, bravo Holmes!' quipped I.

There was an awkward silence.

'Anyway...' said Holmes, 'let me tell you what occurred in your house that night...' And the great detective related the tale of how Sir Gaylon's wicked lust for gold was kindled when he learned about the news of the coronet residing at the house; how he bent Mary to his will and how she protected his identity when she saw you coming downstairs on that evening, on which she closed the window rapidly, and told you about one of the servants' escapades with her woodenlegged lover, which was all perfectly true.

'Your boy, Arthur, went to bed after his interview with you, but he slept badly on account of his uneasiness about his club debts. In the middle of the night he heard a soft tread pass his door, and looking out, was surprised to see his cousin walking very stealthily along the passage, until she disappeared into your dressing room. Petrified with astonishment, the lad slipped on some clothes and waited there in the dark to see what would come of this strange affair. Presently she emerged from the room again, and in the light of the passage lamp your son saw that she carried the precious coronet in her hands. She passed down the stairs, and he, thrilling with horror, ran along and slipped behind the curtain near your door whence he could see what passed in the hall beneath. He saw her open the window, hand out the coronet to someone in the gloom, and then closing it once more hurry back to her own room, passing quite close to where he stood hidden behind the curtain.

'As long as she was on the scene he could not take any action without a horrible exposure of the woman he loved. But the instant she was gone he realised how crushing a misfortune this would be for you, and how all-important it was to set it right. He rushed down, just as he was, in his bare feet, opened the window, sprang out into the snow, and ran down the lane, where he could see a dark figure in the moonlight. Sir Gaylon tried to get away, but Arthur caught him, and there was a struggle between them, your lad tugging at one side of the coronet, and the opponent at the other. In the scuffle, your son struck Sir Gaylon, and cut him over the eye. Then something suddenly snapped, and your son, finding that he had the coronet in his hands, rushed back, closed the window, ascended to your room, and had just observed that the coronet had been twisted in the struggle and was endeavouring to straighten it, when you appeared upon the scene.'

'It is possible?' gasped the banker.

'Certainly it is! You roused his anger by calling him names when he took the chivalrous view and preserved her secret.'

'How cruelly I have misjudged him!'

Holmes and I nodded in unison.

'Where are the gems?'

'You would not think that a thousand pounds apiece an excessive sum for them?'

'I would pay ten.'

'Sold!' I cried.

Holmes sighed and rolled his eyes. 'Three thousand will cover the matter.'

'And there is a reward, I fancy?' I squeaked. 'Four thousand?'

With a dazed face the banker made out another cheque. Holmes walked over to his desk, took out a little triangular piece of gold with three gems in it, and threw it down upon the table. With a shriek of joy and a furious nodding of his head our client clutched it up.

'You have it!' he shouted. 'I am saved! I am saved!'

The reaction of joy was as passionate as his grief had been, and he hugged his recovered gems to his bosom.

'There is one other thing you owe, Mister Holdup,' said Sherlock Holmes, rather sternly.

'Name the sum and I will pay it.'

'No, the debt is not to me. You owe a very humble apology to that noble lad, your son, who has carried himself in this matter as I should be proud to see my own son do, should I ever chance to have one.'

'Then let me hurry to him at once, to let him know that the truth is known.' He gathered himself up in readiness to depart. He thrust out his hand to me.

'Thank you, Doctor Watson,' said he, and then turned to face Holmes. 'And thank you for saving me and England from a great public scandal. Sir, I cannot find the words to thank you, but you shall not find me ungrateful for what you have done. Your skill has exceeded all that I have ever heard of. And now I must fly to apologise to my dear boy for the wrong which I have done him. As to what you tell me of poor Mary, it goes to my heart. Not even your skill can tell me where she is now.'

'I think we may safely say,' returned Holmes, 'that Mary is wherever Sir Gaylon Schwinger is too. It is certain that whatever her sins are, they will soon receive a more than sufficient punishment.'

Punishment? Maybe Holmes had a point I supposed, in the fact that Sir Gaylon was such a rum fellow with girls, cards and the turf that she would receive her just desserts, but my eyes glazed over at the vivid memory of Miss Mary Holdup in the throes of ecstasy, which drew me to the conclusion they might be a good match.

'Holmes,' I said, 'believe me, I have much to tell you about the recent justice in this world.'

'You have suffered by her tongue, Watson, and so will he.'

'I must be off,' said Mr. Holdup, 'and give these beryls to the jeweller for mending.' He donned his hat and shuffled out of the apartment, still badly bruised from our landlady's attentions but with his nodding head held up high and waving his stick joyously as he closed the door. I glanced at Holmes in a ponderous way. He put his hands in his pockets and let out a sigh of satisfaction.

'There goes a man who is his own worst enemy,' said I. 'Someone who could have left the National Treasure in his own secure bank in the heart of the City but, instead, decided to take it to his unfortified home in Streatham and place it in a wafer-thin wooden bureau with a child's lock on it. What a stupid banker.'

'Ah, yes, indeed, Watson. Stupid is as stupid does.'

'He staked his reputation, his honour, his health and his wealth, and the love of his family.'

'But unless he had acted so stupidly, we wouldn't have four thousand pounds.'

'Four thousand plus five hundred for the expenses. We could have another evening of Fanny by Gaslight!'

'Nor would we have found out that our housekeeper is a prostitute.'

'In that respect, my dear Doctor, I believe we are all prostitutes.'